FAMOUS FORRY FOTOS

Kodackerman
Memories

Dedicated to Julie Schwartz
Friend for 70 years

FAMOUS FORRY FOTOS

Over 70 years of AckerMemories

BY

Forrest J Ackerman

Sense of Wonder Press
JAMES A. ROCK & COMPANY, PUBLISHERS
ROCKVILLE • MARYLAND

Famous Forry Fotos
With an introduction by Forrest J Ackerman
Fotos selected by Forrest J Ackerman

is an imprint of *JAMES A. ROCK & CO., PUBLISHERS*

Copyright © 2001 by Forrest J Ackerman

Address comments and inquiries to:
SENSE OF WONDER PRESS
James A. Rock & Company, Publishers
113 N. Washington Street, Box 347
Rockville, MD 20850

E-mail:
jrock@rockpublishing.com   lrock@senseofwonderpress.com
Internet URL: www.SenseOfWonderPress.com

Paperbound ISBN: 0-918736-32-3

Printed in the United States of America
First Sense of Wonder Press Edition: November 2001

CONTENTS

Forry in New York City, 1939, attending the first World Science Fiction Convention: "I thought everyone was coming in costume!"

INTRODUCTION

Just Call Me The Man WITH A Thousand Faces

Hugo Gernsback, Boris Karloff, Robert Bloch, Catherine Moore, Fritz Lang, Wendayne Ackerman, Ray Bradbury, Anne Hardin, Curt Siodmak, Barbara Steele, Isaac Asimov, Vampira, Vincent Price, George Pal, Florence Marley, Ray Harryhausen, Mae Clarke, Richard Matheson, Heidi Saha, Trina Robbins, Jim Warren, Nancy Davis (Reagan), Merian C. Cooper, Tor Johnson . . . see how many faces you can find with mine as I grow older before your eyes.

Forrest J Ackerman

FORRY,
FAMILY & FRIENDS

**Kodackerman
Memories**

Famous Forry Fotos

Alfred Elton van Vogt, 40 years a friend, client and collaborator. Gave me his last autograph.

Bangs for the memories!

Before I became Forrest J Ackerman!

An official portrait at age 4 and a half.

Here I am getting my goat!

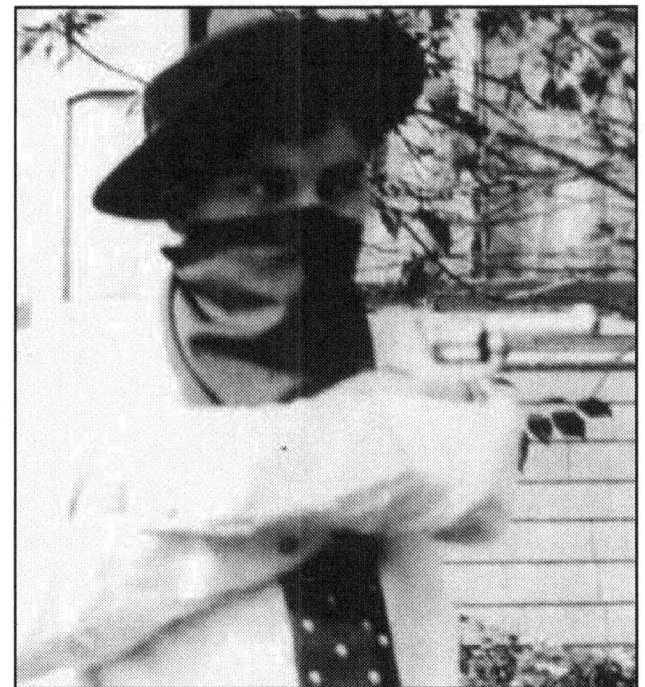

Watch out for Bad Dad!

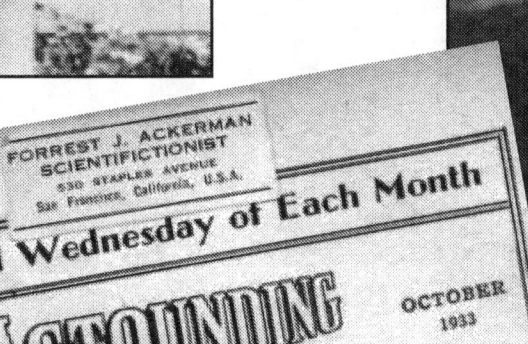

Me in the early 1930s. This is a "futuristicostume" of my own creation. (Foto Mother)

LA home, 5327 Virginia Ave., still there, where I discovered "scientifiction" in October 1926.

Frisco home where I had 117 "stf" (sci-fi) correspondents around the world when I was 15.

A family portrait: brother Alden, my mother, Carroll, Dad William and me at our San Francisco home in 1933. This house at 530 Staples [see foto above] is still there.

Dad with megaphone before mikes. (Foto Gardner Blackman)

A lovely photo of my mother, Carroll.

A candid photo of me just before Pearl Harbor.

The Ackerboys and my girlfriend Tigrina. (Foto by Dad)

As a slender youth at 236½ N. New Hampshire, LA. The apartment is still there. The youth is no longer so young or slender. (Foto Grandfather Wyman)

Tigrina, with whom I collaborated on the Invisibilityarn "The Little Girl Who Wasn't There". (Foto Dad Ackerman)

The terror of World War II. Private Ack-Ack.
(Foto Bruce Yerke)

With Miss Finland of 1945.

S/SGT Ack-Ack of WW II looking
forryward to being a civilian again!

Mother and Dad. He died at 56, she at 94.

Happiest day of my life! Discharged from the Army after 3 years, 4 months, and 29 days of WW II.

Beloved maternal grandmother Belle "Zululu" Wyman. She read me, then reread, entire issues of Ghost Stories Magazine *in the 1920s.*

At the grave of my brother, Alden Lorraine Ackerman
(1923–1945, New Year's Day), in the military cemetery
on the outskirts of Luxembourg.

Ackerman and Ackerwoman, England, 1951. I'm wearing a copy of an Al Jolson sweater she had made for me. (Foto Eric Frank Russell)

Wendy and I, she in the Lincoln chair. Note Dracula, Mummy rings on my fingers. (Foto Daugherty)

Wearing character glasses of Lon Chaney Sr. (Foto Lincoln Bond)

Cut out of my cameo in THE POWER. But so was its producer George Pal!

Looking at Eve in Adam. (Foto Bill Rotsler)

Eek, look before you leak! Papparazzi foto by Dik Daniels. (His mysterious death directly thereafter by aggravated Twonk's Disease—fallen armpits—has never been Acksplained)

Made up by young teen Paul Clemens as Dr. Phibes. His mother, actress Eleanor Parker, starred with Charlton Heston in the George Pal movie THE NAKED JUNGLE based on "Leiningen vs. the Ants" (real sci-ants fiction).

Mary Ellen Rabogliatti-Daugherty halps me celebrate a brrrrthday. (Foto Wendayne Ackerman)

The sci-fi-mobile, 65th birthday gift of a Cadillackermobile from Jim Warren. Eventually given to Brian Forbes years later when I got a new Lincoln. I thought he'd preserve it as a memento. He sold it!

A favorite foto. (Dunno know who to thank for taking it.)

My Mother and legendary Weird Tales author Bassett Morgan. I seem to have been the only one who ever sought her out.

They called me chicken because I had Bela's cape on (capon). (Foto Lincoln Bond)

ScientiClaus Efjay

Dial 323-MOON FAN. Universal Studios. (Foto Art Saha)

Early 40s' 4E. Green-rimmed "phantom" glasses. (Foto Morojo)

Fatso Forry Passport Foto 1951.

As I see myself. (And as photographer Jay Kay Klein captured me.)

Lugosi's Dracula ring (carnelian with silver overlay). (Foto Daugherty)

An orange peel never had it so bad. (Foto Brian Forbes)

Caught offguard, the real me.

Any volunteers?

*I meet
my
Ackerclone.
(Foto
Daugherty)*

Los Angeles Mayor Tom Bradley's Commendation.

Mayor Tom Bradley accepting my collection for the city of Los Angeles but nothing came of it.

FORREST J ACKERMAN
Presents

VOICE
OF THE
IMAGI-NATION

TECHNICAL DIRECTOR
PRODUCED BY
BRIAN L. FORBES   JOSEPH D. VALDEZ

DIRECTED BY
WILLIAM R. WINTERSOLE   FICTIONAL CONSULTANTS
HOWARD DEVORE
STEPHEN WARD
ASSOCIATE PRODUCER   KENNETH ANGER
MICHAEL P. HODEL

MUSIC BY
KENNETH STRICKFADEN

STORIES SELECTED
AND INTRODUCED BY
FORREST J ACKERMAN

STARRING

WILLIAM WINTERSOLE
MICHAEL HODEL
ANN ROBINSON
ANGUS SCRIMM
ALFA-BETTY OLSEN
MARSHALL EFRON
MARTINE BESWICK
EDWARD ANSARA
CAMILLE KEATON
AND OTHERS

KPFK FM 90.7 LOS ANGELES

PRODUCED THROUGH
THE BELLEROPHON NETWORK
IN ASSOCIATION WITH
PACIFICA FOUNDATION RADIO

But it never materialized, lost in the Realm of Unwrought Things.

FORRY
FANDOM

Kodackerman
Memories

Famous Forry Fotos

PROJECT 6000/8700

Project 6000 grew to 8700 as wife Wendayne & I toured the country to visit as many of the 1300 filmonster fans as we could who wanted to see us. I'm still in contact with Gary Dorst, Jerry Weist, Mark Frank and James Warren. One fan promised me if I'd visit him he'd have 50 for me so we went 35 miles out of our way to Niles, Mich., where we were met by one boy … and 49 sheep! The Lon Chaney star is on Hollywood Blvd.

Meeting Jerry Weist on the 8700-mile fan trip.

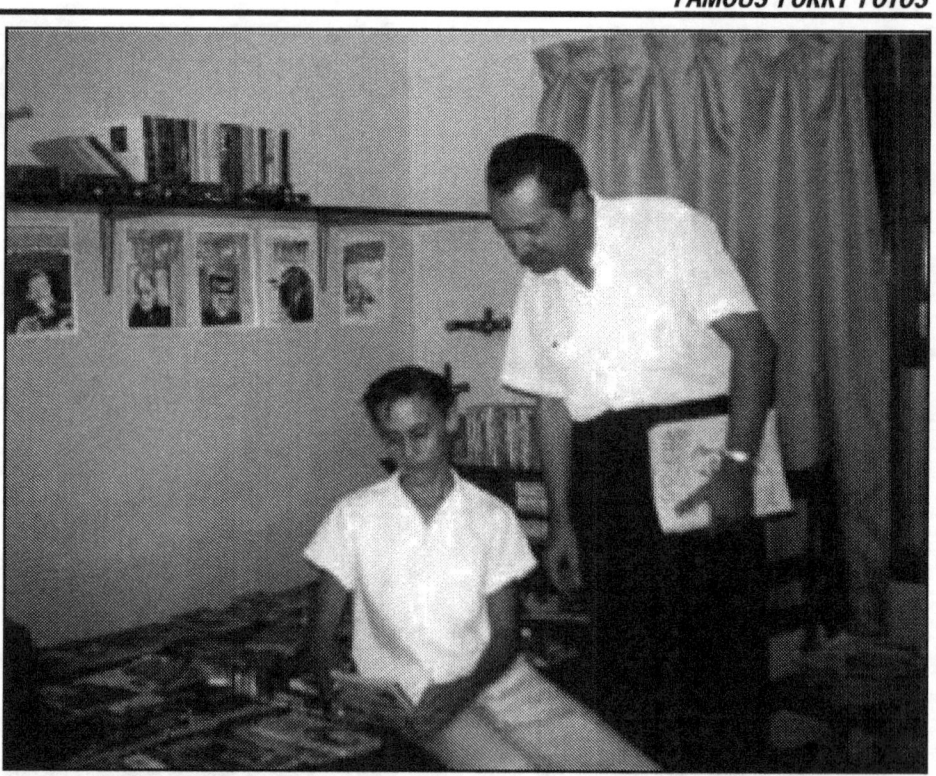

A reception in Ohio, 1963, during our 8700-mile cross country trip.

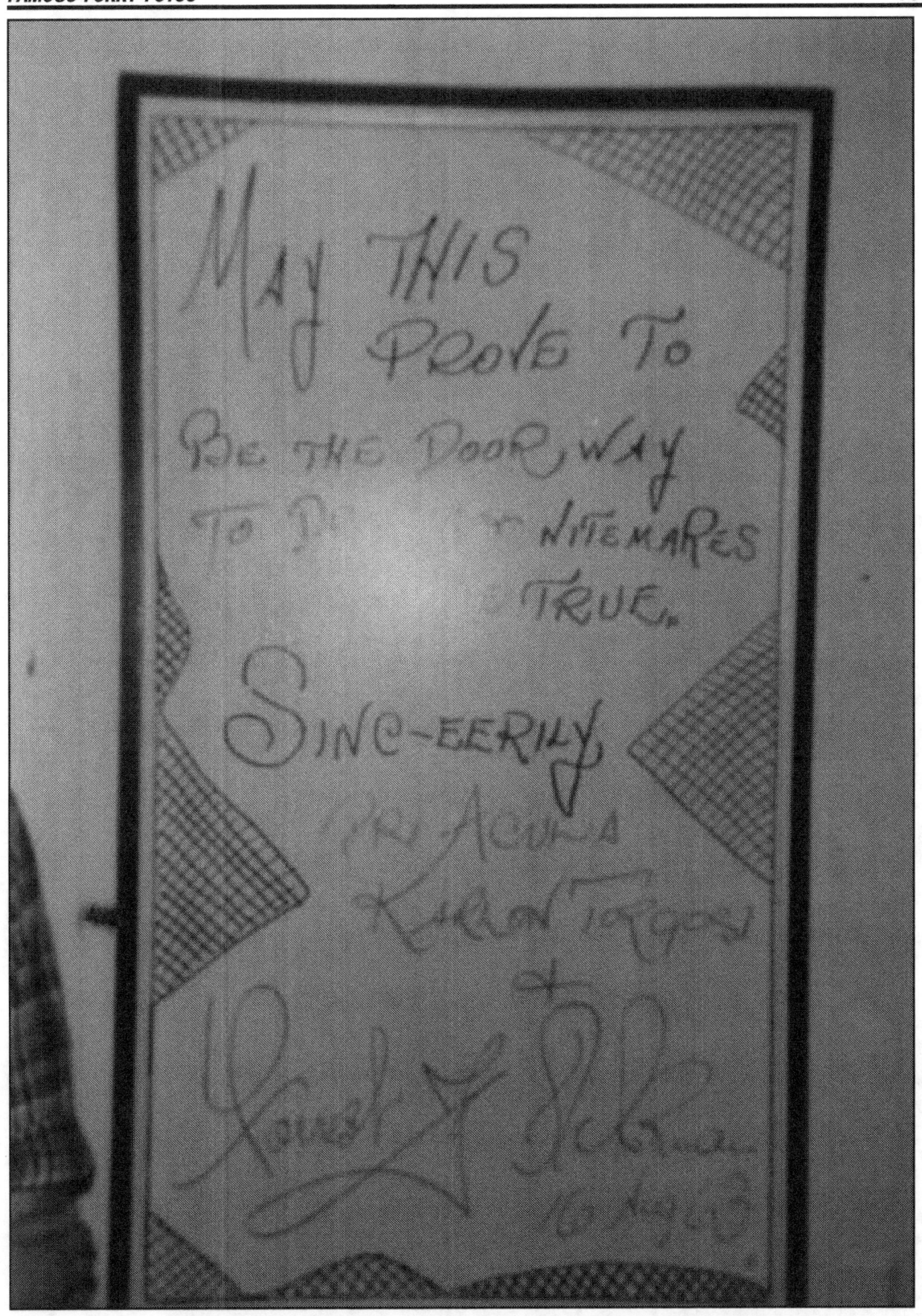

At their request I signed the door to their private theater in the home of young fans
during the 8700-mile tour: "May this prove to be the doorway to Dreams and Nitemares
come true. Sinc-eerily Dr. Acula Karlon Torgosi & Forrest J Ackerman, 16 Aug 63."

Mike mine a double.
(Foto Daugherty)

Famous Monsters Convention 1965.
(Foto Daugherty)

It's not easy being an Ackermonster. Original Famous Monsters Convention, NYC.
(Foto Daugherty)

Hey, guys, how come you looked at this picture first? Haven't you ever seen Bob Bloch and me before? Oh, the luminous fanne is Amy Jewett. Sorry she's married, wolves, and with 2 children.

First Fandom Fan Dave Kyle as Ming the Merciless at a World SF Convention Masquerade. John Michel directly behind him.

Chinese baby face. I hope she sees this and reminds me of her name. (Foto Bjo Trimble)

Sometimes a fan like this will introduce himself to me as a grown man.

Ion Hobana, #1 fan of Romania. He thinks of himself as my younger brother and we love each other like siblings.

Japanfan Betibupiko.

"Boris Karloff is dead."
Heart-breaking
announcement to
members of Count
Dracula Society, after
Dark Sunday, 2 February
1959. (Foto Daugherty)

Speaking at a Count
Dracula Society fanquet.
(Foto by Daugherty)

35

Beauties & the Beast (brunet Angelique Trouvere, blond "Animal". (Foto Daugherty)

Kristina Hallind, #1 fan of Sweden. (Foto Wendayne Ackerman)

The mail in my livingroom when I returned from a 75-day trip abroad, 1965. The hands look familiar. (Foto Daugherty)

The Vertileb brothers, now adults, big monster fans of mine to this day.

MONSTERS & ALIENS

**Kodackerman
Memories**

Famous Forry Fotos

Famous Forry Fotos

Famous Forry Fotos

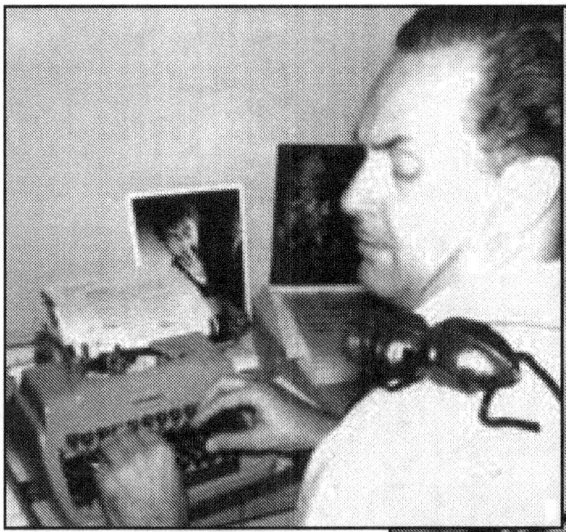

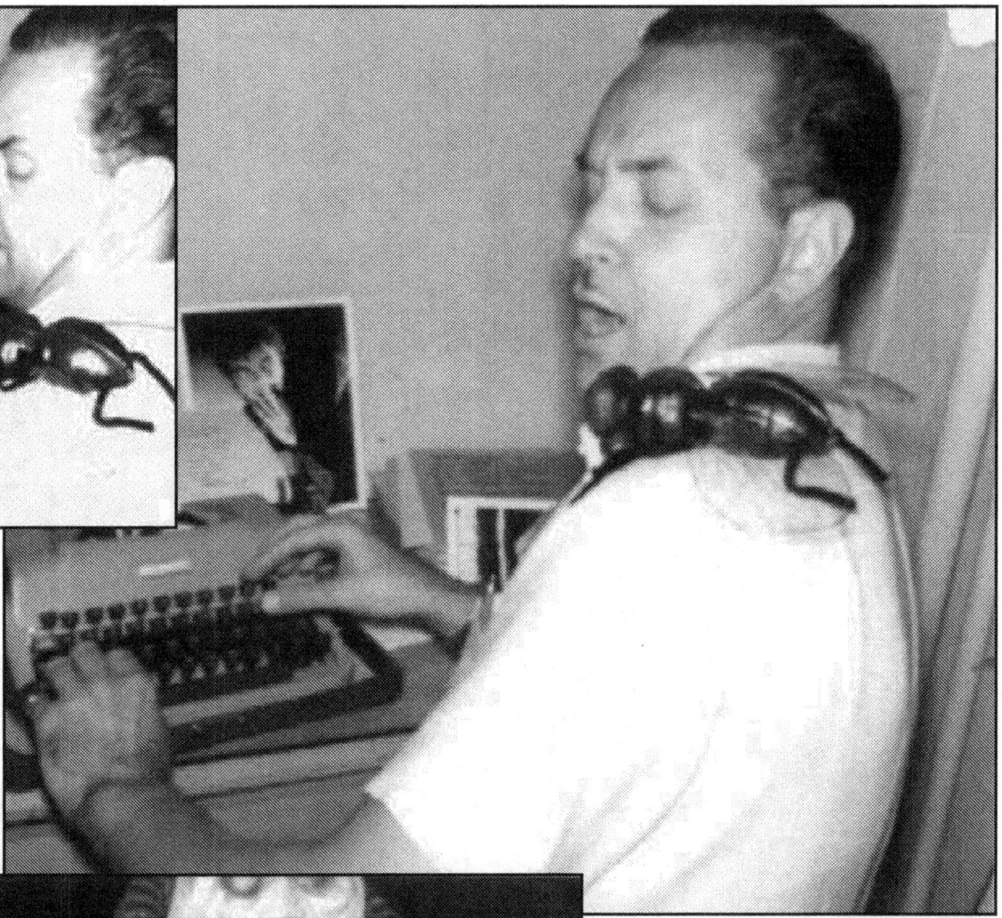

Editing the original Famous Monsters of Filmland, early 60s, NYC.

Attacked by Nightmares.

Nearly losing a finger in 1967.

In Joe Blasco's Studio.

42

"You say WHAT has escaped from the Black Lagoon?" Joe Blasco Makeup Center.

Xtine Lyons woos my Outer Limits monster.

Son of Donovan's Brain. (Foto Daugherty)

I'd walk a million miles for one of your smiles, My Mummy! (Al Jolson)

*Two
Happy
Monsters.*

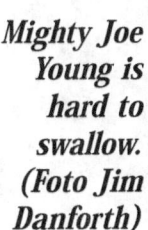

*Mighty Joe
Young is
hard to
swallow.
(Foto Jim
Danforth)*

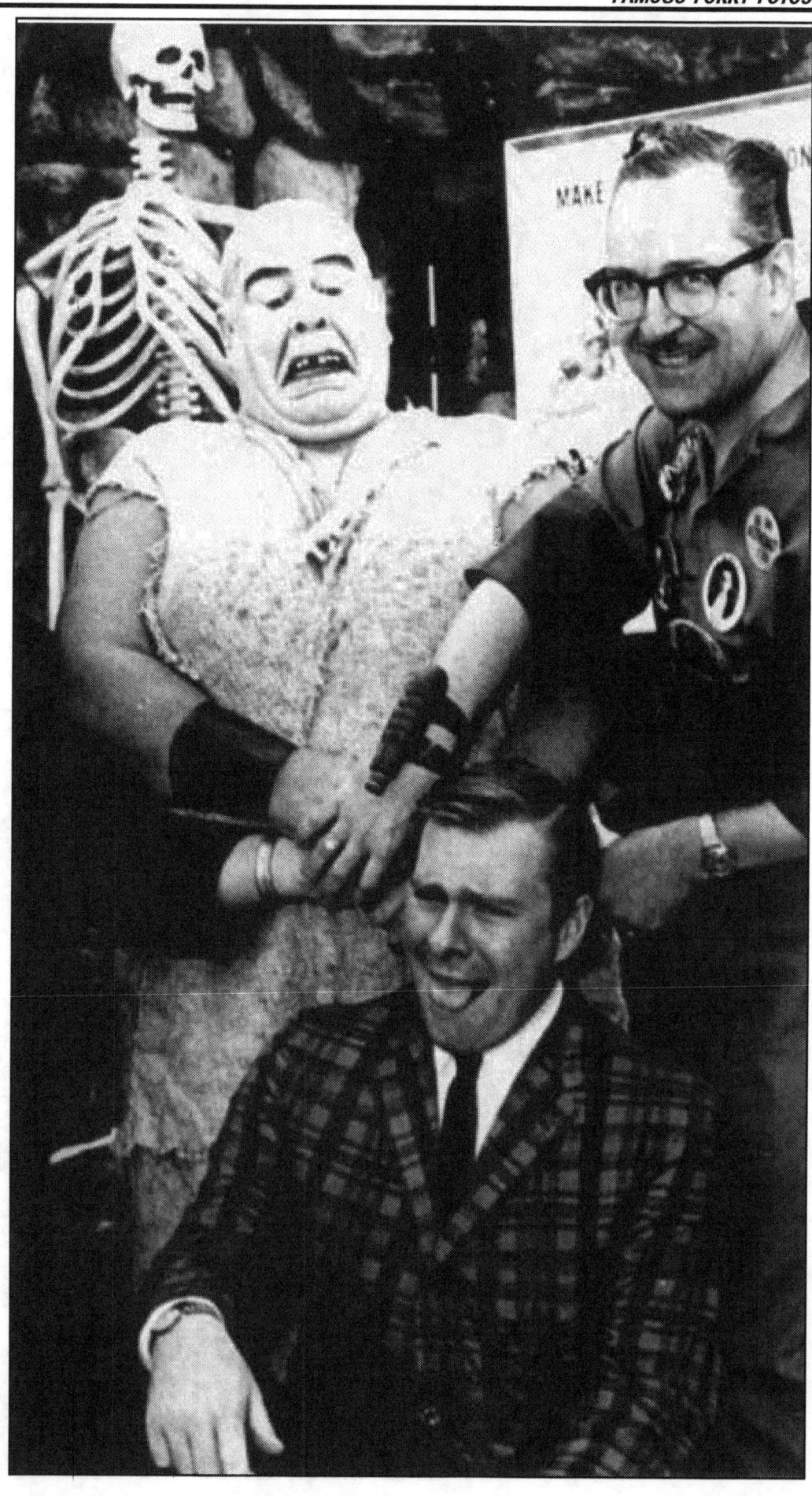

Tor "Lobo" Johnson and I attack Verne Langdon.

Rick Baker's Kong at (Grau) Mann's Chinese Forecourt attended by Fay Wray, Ray Harryhausen, Ray Bradbury, Rich Correll, John Landis, Hugh Hefner and—who he?

Saucer Man vs. Saucy Man.

I'm dancing with fears in my eyes 'cuz the ghoul in my arms isn't you.

The Inscription reads "To Forry with every best wish." Ray Harryhausen has been my dear friend for 60 years. His first animodel brontosaurus is in the Ackermuseum.

I saw this in 1939 when I attended the first World Science Fiction Convention in New York and visited the World Fair there.

I found Frankenstein! On the outskirts of Erlanger, KY, headed toward LA. (Foto Wendayne Ackerman)

Ackermonster goes to bat for Sandy Claws. (Foto Daugherty)

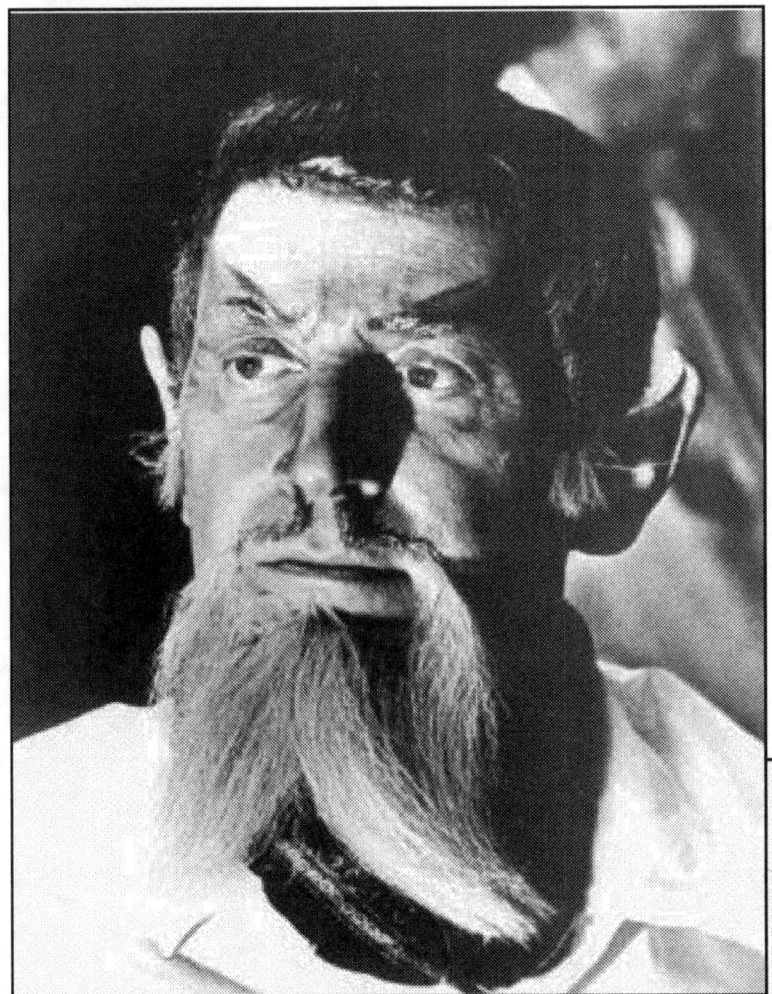

Made up by Tony Tierney. Wendy opened the door on this unexpected Ackermonster ... and screamed! (Foto by Tierney)

Surrounded by friendly UFO aliens created by Bjo Trimble.

FORRY'S
TRAVELS

**Kodackerman
Memories**

Foto by LIFE magazine in 1951 when I was about to depart on the Queen Mary to be Guest of Honour in London at the First International Science Fiction Convention. Wearing Green Phantom fashion glasses.

At the chalet in Switzerland where Mary Wollstonecraft Shelley dreamed up Frankenstein. (Foto Wendayne Ackerman)

Legendary London address.

Me in Rome. (Note misspelling of Jon Hall, in whose home I now live).

With George Langelaan, author of "The Fly", in his home in Paris.

Receiving my Italian Hugo.

LA BELLE ET LA BETE, seen in the Cinematheque Francais in Paris. (Foto Sig Wahrman)

Nordkapp, Norway, 1000 miles from the North Pole, at midnight in the Land of the Midnight Sun. (Foto Sig Wahrman)

In the Paris Cinematheque. (Foto Sig Wahrman)

Gorgeous attire worn by star in 1922 French version of L'ATLANTIDE (ATLANTIS). French filmuseum, Paris. (Foto Sig Wahrman)

At the George Méllès Tribute somewhere in Europe. I've forrygotten. (Foto Curt Siodmak)

CELEBRITIES, FRIENDS & FIENDS

**Kodackerman
Memories**

Famous Forry Fotos

The Martian Chronicler, Lifelong Friend of Dr. Acula.

Julius Schwartz, Sam Moskowitz, FJA, Dave Kyle, Conrad H. Ruppert (Foto John L. Coker II)

Unpublished 3-dimensional portrait of The Bride of Frankenstein and "Mad Love" Lorre by Albert Nuetzell.

With artist Anton Brzezinski.

Spock speaks, Efjay listens.

Famous Monsters cover artist Albert Nuetzell.

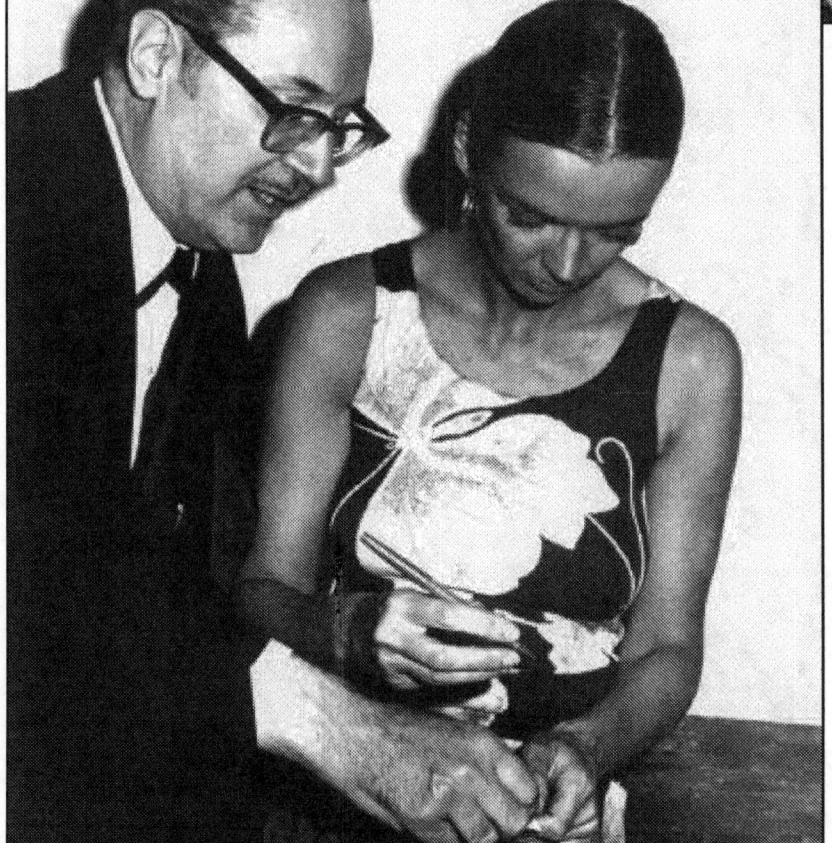

Barbara Steeles the show from me. (Foto Walt Daugherty)

Look hard—can you pick out Florence Marley, Bill Nolan, Tigrina, Ib Melchior, Carroll Borland, Terri Merritt-Pinckard, Bill Warren, Ray Russell, A.E. van Vogt, Bjo Trimble, Donald Reed, Kris Neville, Alex Gordon ... but where am I? Is it possible I took the picture?

Sci-fi Writers Conference Dublin 1976 with Theo. Sturgeon, Brian W. Aldiss, Fred Pohl, Harry Harrison, Anne MacCaffrey, Gordon Dickson, Raymond Z. Gallun and can you spot a 25-year younger FJA?

With Christopher Lee and Walter Ernsting, creator of Perry Rhodan. (Foto Wendayne Ackerman)

Frankenforry & the Blind Hermit Walt Daugherty (makeups by Mary Ellen Rabogliatti-Daugherty) with the author of "The Four-sided Triangle", William F. Temple, and his wife Joan. (Foto by Mrs. Daugherty)

Hugo Gernsback, the Father of Science Fiction, with the Son, 4E Ackerman. (Foto Ruth Landis/ Kyle)

With Hope Lugosi, Bela's last wife.

Terri Merritt-Pinckard, author of "Monsters are <u>Good</u> for My Children". (Foto Dik Daniels)

My Collaborator Anne Hardin & Me.

Kongratulating Merian C. Cooper.

Anthony Boucher, author of "Rocket to the Morgue".

Actress Vikki Dougan, the Backless Dress Sensation of 1957.

My "Nyusa/ Yvala" collaborator Catherine Louise Moore. (Foto Daugherty)

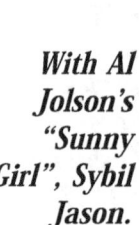

With Al Jolson's "Sunny Girl", Sybil Jason.

Dear Jack Williamson, whose first sf story, "The Metal Man", I still remember reading in 1928. His beloved wife tragically died in an auto accident. Mine died as the aftermath of a mugging in Naples.

I'll string along with you, Carrolluna Borland. In her home the day we met. (Foto Daugherty)

Friend/client Martin Varno, scripter of NIGHT OF THE BLOOD BEAST. His father, Roland Varno, spoke the only lines in English to Marlene Dietrich in DER BLAUE ENGEL (THE BLUE ANGEL). And I believe he appeared in one vampire film but I have a Senior moment on it as I type. Ask Bill Warren, he can probably tell you (being a junior).

With Trina, the artist who threw the threads on Vampirella.

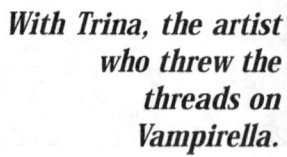

A proud moment with my friend Fritz METROPOLIS Lang at a Count Dracula banquet with Karl THE MUMMY Freund, John Countless Horror Films Carradine, Vincent DR PHIBES Price and numerous other celebrities present, including Donald A. Reed, Walt Daugherty, Miss Science Fiction Gayna Shireen and Wendayne Ackerman.

Presenting Robert Bloch with his ASYLUM award, 1972. (Foto Daugherty)

On my 50th birthday with Florence QUEEN OF BLOOD Marley.

With John Carradine with whom I appeared in THE HOWLING.

In the home of Lon Chaney Sr.'s brother.

William (BLACULA) Marshall.

Richard Sheffield, Bela Lugosi's closest friend the last 3 years of his life.

Who does she look like a female version of? That's right, she's Peter Lorre's daughter. With Jim Warren. Unfortunately, like her famous father she's passed on.

I had a crush on her 55 years ago. Laurel Lee Donn. Do you blame me?

Vampira vamps me.

Carroll Borland and daughter Anne Parten, looking like a recreation of her mother as Luna.

Post, Lee, me, Harryhausen, Langdon.

Lurk alikes Vincent & Efjay.

My Pal George. I gave the eulogy at his huge Hollywood funeral. His "bride", as he always called her, Szoka, in the background. His memory is honored annually by an award from the Academy of Science Fiction, Fantasy & Horror Films. (Foto Daugherty)

Curt (DONOVAN'S BRAIN) Siodmak, receiving a Gernsback Award; I knew him for 60 years. (Foto Daugherty)

Receiving the FIRST Hugo from the hands of Isaac Asimov, World SF Con,
1953, Philadelphia. To my left, Olga & Willy Ley, he the great rocket expert
as well as sci-fi author writing under the name Robert Willey.

Dear friend, client and special friend of Hannes Bok, Emil Petaja.

What's so funny, honey?

Heidi Saha as Vampirella.

The day Boris Karloff recorded the Decca Record Album I scripted, 1968, "An Evening with Boris Karloff and His Friends".

At the Magic Castle in Horrorwood. Front row is Lee and me.
Back row is Robert Bloch, his wife Elly, and Wendy.

MOVIES & TELEVISION

**Kodackerman
Memories**

Famous Forry Fotos

My Ackademy Award (teehee) death scene in DRACULA VS. FRANKENSTEIN.

*Ill-fated
Wasp
Woman
Susan
Cabot,
murdered
by her son
… but not
before she
kissed me.*

*With director Rouben
Mamoulian, who gave us
Fredric March's DR. JEKYLL &
MR. HYDE.*

*Brinke
Stevens as
Luna of
MARK OF
THE
VAMPIRE
hypnotized
by Dr. Acula.*

Charles Grodin
& Jessica Lang
on set of
DeLaurentiis'
KING WRONG.

J. Carrol Naish on
set of DRACULA VS.
FRANKENSTEIN.

93

Queen of Blood Velana (Florence Marley) and the Voice of the Xtaby, Yma Sumac, with the blob from Outer Limits' "Don't Open Till Doomsday". (Foto Bill Rotsler)

Florence Marley, Queen of Blood.

With the beaver hat Lon Chaney wore in the lost film LONDON AFTER MIDNIGHT. Gift of Philip J. Riley. (Foto Daugherty)

With Esperantista aktoro Lew Ayres on the set of DONOVAN'S BRAIN, 1952. (Foto Tom Gries)

Actress Nancy Davis before she became the First Lady, Nancy Reagan. On the set of the second of 3 versions of DONOVAN'S BRAIN.

Joan Shawlee of George Pal's CONQUEST OF SPACE.

With Ann Robinson, heroine of WAR OF THE WORLDS.

Metropolis, My Home Town. (Colored city by Albert Nuetzell)

Richard Matheson who scripted and had a cameo in SOMEWHERE IN TIME.

With the Lord High Minister of All that was Sinister on the set of THE RAVEN.

With Elsa THE BRIDE OF FRANKENSTEIN Lanchester & Donald A. Reed (Foto Walt Daugherty)

Mae Clarke, the original bride of Dr. Frankenstein. (Foto Walt Daugherty)

An autograph from the Bride of Frankenstein, Elsa Lanchester. (Foto Wendayne Ackerman)

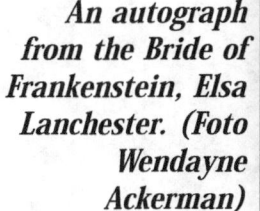

Lori Nelson and the beast from THE DAY THE WORLD ENDED regard Swedish sci-fi mag with me.

The planetary ape looks like he's about to ... go ape! (Foto Daugherty)

On the set of the Vincent Price TV Horror Hail of Fame.

Holding the head of Schlock on the set of TV's Horror Hall of Fame special.

Academy Award Winner William Tuttle Faces His Greatest Challenge during shooting of TV Special "Horror Hall of Fame" to change the Ackermonster (FJA) into Ghouldilocks.

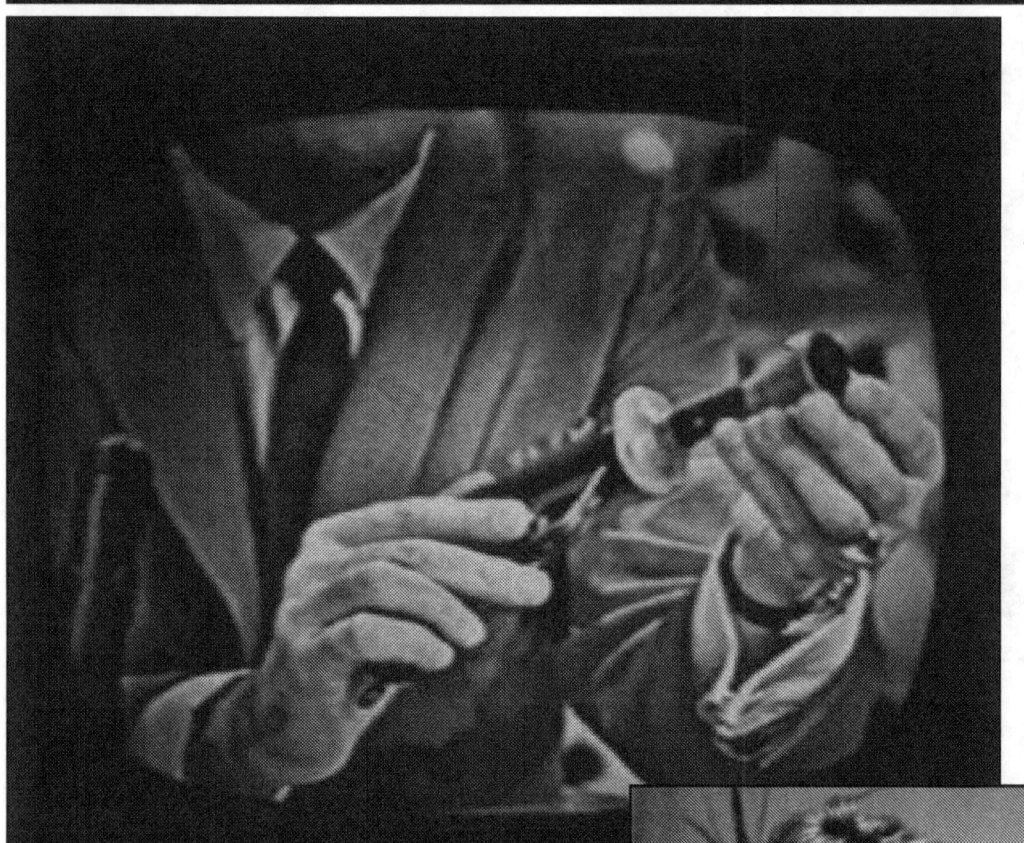

With Buck Rogers' zapgun from 1930s on Japanese TV.

Made up for TV.

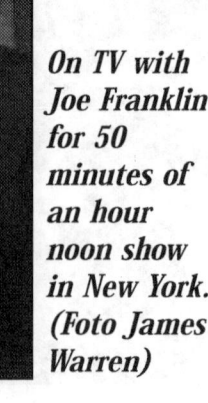

On TV with Joe Franklin for 50 minutes of an hour noon show in New York. (Foto James Warren)

One of my early TV appearances. (Fotos Sig Wahrman)

THE ACKERMANSION

**Kodackerman
Memories**

Famous Forry Fotos

*Aftermath
of
earthquake.*

*The sign on the original
Ackermansion at 915 S. Spaceborn,
er, Sherbourne Drive. Now, alas, an
apartment building.*

*Typical
scene at
my work
desk.*

Life Masks.
Lower row (right to left):
Glenn Strange, Peter Lorre,
Don Post,
Charles Laughton.
Middle Row:
John Carradine,
Tor Johnson, Lon Jr.,
Vincent Price.
Top Row:
Centered between Boris and
Bela is me when
I was alive.

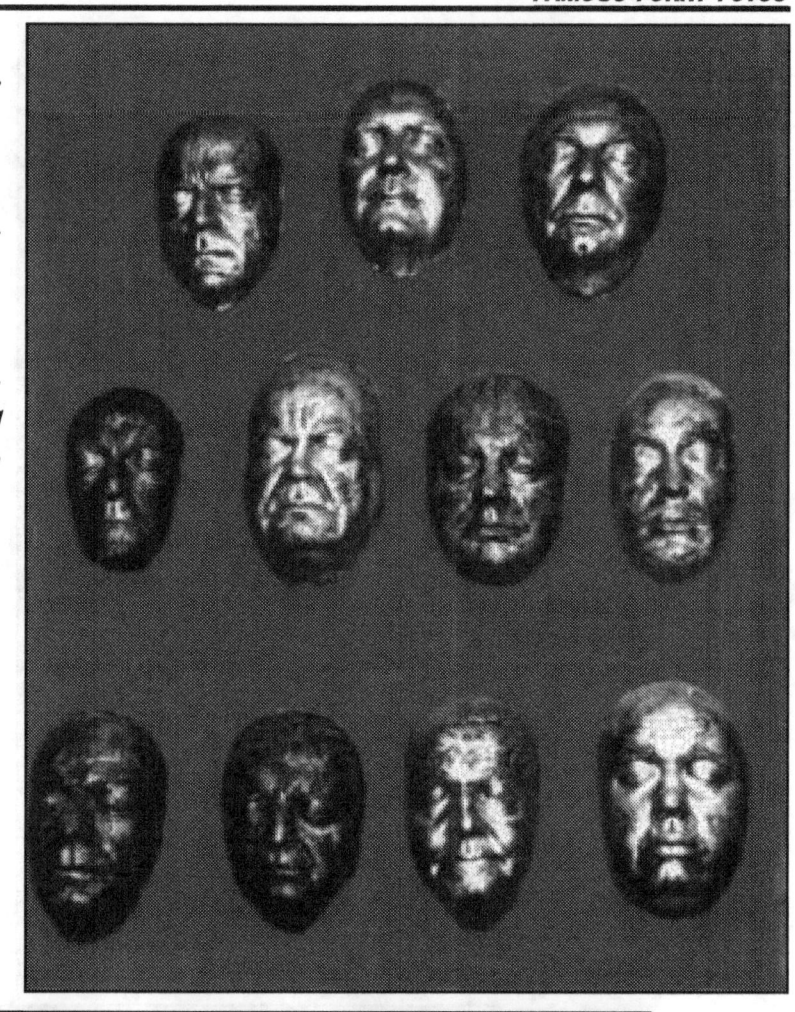

Dining Room shot in original
Ackermansion with Wendayne for BBC/TV.

On a sliding panel covering books in my office.

Dictating to my secretary, Lori Birmingham. (Foto Wendayne Ackerman.)

Like Nature I abhor a vacuum. You won't catch me at work like this nowadays.

Gotta move all this to son of Ackermansion?!

Guests in the old Ackermansion. Couple to left, fans Florence & Sam (Mr. and Mrs.) Russell.

With DracuLee, early 70s.

Academy Award winner Dennis Muren visiting me in the Ackermansion.

THE MAD GHOUL, David Bruce, in the Daugherty Room of the Ackermansion shortly before his death.

Inclined to take it easy.

50,000 books and counting. (Yes, I've read every last word. When I get a new book I turn to the last page and ...)

With Shel Dorf in my patio with half the ATLANTIS, THE LOST CONTINENT submarine stolen some years ago. (Foto Walt Daugherty)

Fan gathering at the original Ackermansion. (Foto Wendayne Ackerman)

FORRY's HOUSE AGAIN, 1970.

Wecome to the original Ackermansion. Space montage by Morris Scott Dollens. (Foto Wendayne Ackerman)

Driveway to the garage of the original Ackermansion.

The End

Capricious moment of Wendayne captured by her first lover, Paul Strumpfl, when she was still Matylda Malka Wahrmann. I thought of contacting her by ouija board to see if it was okay with her to publish this picture but then I realized that she, like me, didn't believe in a hereafter. I'm sure this fun-loving free soul would say "Okay, Forile" (pronounced Fori-luh, her pet German name for me), even though as, like me, Marlene Dietrich, Katherine Hepburn, Carl Sagan, Isaac Asimov, Gene Roddenberry, H.G. Wells and other nonbelievers she didn't have a soul. Here's looking at you, Wendy, wherever you aren't.

www.ingramcontent.com/pod-product-compliance
Lightning Source LLC
Chambersburg PA
CBHW080833250626
47160CB00008B/2923